INSIDE

DC
UNITED

BY SAM MOUSSAVI

SportsZone

abdobooks.com

Published by Abdo Publishing, a division of ABDO, PO Box 398166, Minneapolis, Minnesota 55439. Copyright © 2022 by Abdo Consulting Group, Inc. International copyrights reserved in all countries. No part of this book may be reproduced in any form without written permission from the publisher. SportsZone™ is a trademark and logo of Abdo Publishing.

Printed in the United States of America, North Mankato, Minnesota
052021
092021

THIS BOOK CONTAINS
RECYCLED MATERIALS

Cover Photo: Eric Canha/Cal Sport Media/AP Images
Interior Photos: Simon Bruty/Sports Illustrated/SetNumber: X51576/Getty Images, 4–5, 7, 10; Matthew Ashton/EMPICS/PA Images/Getty Images, 8–9, 35, 37; Ed Nessen/AP Images, 13; Shutterstock Images, 15; Brian P. Irwin/Shutterstock Images, 16–17; E. J. Flynn/AP Images, 19; Gerald Herbert/AP Images, 20; Andrew Harnik/AP Images, 23; Tim Sloan/AFP/Getty Images, 25; Harry S. Cahill/AFP/Getty Images, 27; Nick Wass/AP Images, 28, 32, 39; Roberto Candia/AP Images, 31; Chris Carlson/AP Images, 40; Alex Brandon/AP Images, 43

Editor: Patrick Donnelly
Series Designer: Dan Peluso

Library of Congress Control Number: 2019954322

Publisher's Cataloging-in-Publication Data

Names: Moussavi, Sam, author.
Title: DC United / by Sam Moussavi
Description: Minneapolis, Minnesota : Abdo Publishing, 2022 | Series: Inside MLS |
      Includes online resources and index.
Identifiers: ISBN 9781532192555 (lib. bdg.) | ISBN 9781644945643 (pbk.) |
      ISBN 9781098210458 (ebook)
Subjects: LCSH: D.C. United (Soccer team)--Juvenile literature. | Soccer teams--Juvenile
      literature. | Professional sports franchises--Juvenile literature. | Sports Teams--
      Juvenile literature.
Classification: DDC 796.334--dc23

TABLE OF
CONTENTS

CHAPTER 1

A CHAMPIONSHIP
FIRST

Professional soccer was hit or miss in the United States for many years. Leagues came and went, as did fans. Even Major League Soccer (MLS), which debuted in 1996, was no sure thing. The new league needed to get off to a strong start. DC United, one of the original 10 teams, helped set that foundation.

It didn't take long for DC United to become a force in the new league. One season was all it took, in fact. DC boasted a balanced attack with aggressive forwards Raúl Díaz Arce and Jaime Moreno, plus midfielders Marco Etcheverry and John Harkes. Jeff Agoos and Eddie Pope combined with goalkeeper Mark Simpson to lead a sound defense. Together they led United to the third-best record in the league.

DC United's Jaime Moreno (9) fights off the Galaxy's Arash Noamouz during the 1996 MLS Cup.

DC then advanced through the playoffs to reach the MLS Cup, the league's championship match.

Another strong and balanced team, the Los Angeles Galaxy, awaited. DC United finished second in the Eastern Conference, while the Galaxy finished best in the west. Both squads had their share of star players from around the world. And both had won four straight postseason matches to earn a chance to play for the championship.

On October 20, 1996, the teams met in Foxborough, Massachusetts, to determine the league's first champion in the MLS Cup.

FAMILIAR FOES

With only 10 teams in the league in 1996, no MLS squads were strangers to one another. During the regular season the Galaxy and United faced off three times, with the Galaxy winning twice. Led by striker Eduardo Hurtado, the Galaxy had a high-powered offense in 1996. United's defense would have its work cut out in the title match.

The weather would be a challenge for both squads, however. Hurricane Lili brought violent gusts of wind and powerful rainstorms to the New England area.

The match was played on a drenched field, as United star Marco Etcheverry discovered the hard way.

The championship match was almost postponed due to the rough weather conditions. MLS officials decided to play it as scheduled, however, as long as there was no lightning. The quality of the field was a different matter. A water-soaked

A group of DC United fans showed their optimism before the match.

playing surface at Foxboro Stadium would be a major challenge for both squads.

The rough weather didn't stop 34,643 fans from showing up for the championship match. It was also the first MLS championship to be broadcast on national TV in the United States. The match held importance internationally too. So much so that the press box at Foxboro Stadium was filled beyond its capacity. Reporters from all over the globe were forced to

watch the match from the stands. A small group of loyal United fans even traveled up from Washington, DC. About one-third of the crowd was there to support United.

Los Angeles took control of the championship match early on. The Galaxy created several scoring chances within the first few minutes. DC United was on its heels early, and five minutes into the match, Hurtado scored to give the Galaxy a 1–0 lead. DC was able to create a few scoring chances of its own during

DC United's Mario Gori, *right*, races for the ball.

the rest of the first half. But none of the chances led to goals. Los Angeles went into halftime with a 1–0 lead and clear control of the final match.

The Galaxy held on to that momentum early in the second half. Midfielder Chris Armas scored an unassisted goal early in the second half to give the Galaxy a 2–0 lead. Much like the first half, that quick goal put DC United on the defensive.

THE COMEBACK BEGINS

The DC defense held on for the next 15 minutes, preventing the Galaxy from expanding their lead. Then DC's fortunes changed in the 73rd minute. Substitute midfielder Tony Sanneh scored the team's first goal to make the score 2–1. The momentum was starting to shift, but United's job was not finished.

Eight minutes later, another substitute made a huge play. DC midfielder Shawn Medved scored on a rebound from the left side of the net. Just like that, the MLS Cup was tied.

DC actually had more chances to win the match in regulation but could not score. The first MLS Cup would go into overtime. MLS rules stated that overtime matches would be decided by sudden death—or "golden goal" in soccer.

This meant that the first team to score in overtime would win the match.

The Galaxy had a few early chances in the overtime period but could not get the ball in the net. United goalkeeper Simpson stood tall in the face of big pressure from LA.

ONE YEAR, TWO TROPHIES

DC United doubled up as champs in 1996. Ten days after beating Los Angeles in the MLS Cup, DC defeated the Rochester Rhinos in the US Open Cup. The US Open Cup is a knockout tournament that takes place between MLS teams and those playing at lower levels, including amateur teams, from around the United States.

Then in the fourth minute of overtime, MLS history was made. Etcheverry set up for a United corner kick from the left side. After he put the ball in play, teammate Pope swooped in and headed the ball into the back of the net.

DC United was the first champion of Major League Soccer. Etcheverry was named the game's Most Valuable Player (MVP). The dramatic finish cemented his and Pope's place in DC United history. The team's feat in 1996 set the stage for one of the most successful decades in MLS history.

Raúl Díaz Arce holds the trophy after DC United won the first-ever MLS Cup.

CHAPTER 2

A CAPITAL
DYNASTY

While soccer thrived around the world, the sport had long struggled to take off in the United States. The global soccer community wanted to change that, so organizers awarded the hosting right to the 1994 World Cup to the United States. However, one of the conditions for granting those rights was that the US Soccer Federation had to form a new, top-level professional league in the United States.

That new league was called Major League Soccer. On June 15, 1994, Washington, DC, was awarded a founding franchise in MLS. The next step was for team management to choose a name. Some of the options were the Spies, Americans, and Eagles. None of those names stuck, however. Ownership eventually settled on a cleaner name: DC United.

A number of different names were rejected before the club adopted the name DC United.

RFK Stadium hosted DC United home games for 22 seasons.

The name celebrated DC's status as the nation's capital while also paying tribute to famous European clubs such as Manchester United.

From 1996 to 2017, DC United played its home matches at Robert F. Kennedy (RFK) Stadium. The stadium was located in the city's historic seventh ward. Built in 1961, the stadium had once been home to Washington's professional football and baseball teams. By 1996, however, RFK had the historic feel of a classic sports stadium because it didn't have many fancy

extra features. The stadium ended up as the perfect place for United's rabid fanbase.

DC United's early success gave its fans many reasons to cheer. A strong home-field advantage was key to DC United bringing home the league's initial MLS Cup in 1996. The team won 15 of 20 matches played at RFK that year.

GOING BACK TO BACK

United had another strong year in 1997. The team stormed to the MLS Cup again, this time against the Colorado Rapids.

DC United aimed to be the first dynasty in MLS history, and a 2–1 victory over the Rapids went a long way toward making that a reality.

The 1997 season was memorable for many different reasons. Including the playoffs, DC United scored 70 goals in 1997. Many of DC's stars came into their own that year. And DC United's fans creating an intimidating atmosphere at RFK only added to the franchise's reputation.

United boasted unique star power in its early years. Talented South American players such as Marco Etcheverry and Jaime Moreno combined with US national team stars including Eddie Pope, John Harkes, Jeff Agoos, and Tony Sanneh. Forward Roy Lassiter was among the league's best scorers. The team was both balanced and star-studded. United fell short of a third straight MLS Cup win in 1998, losing to the Chicago Fire in the final. But many of the original members of the Black and Red were still around in 1999 when United coasted to its third title in four years. After winning the MLS Cup in 1996, 1997, and 1999, DC United cemented its place in MLS history.

"Three out of four, you can't complain," said Bruce Arena, who coached United in its first three seasons. "Would have been nice to have four out of four, but that's life, you know?"

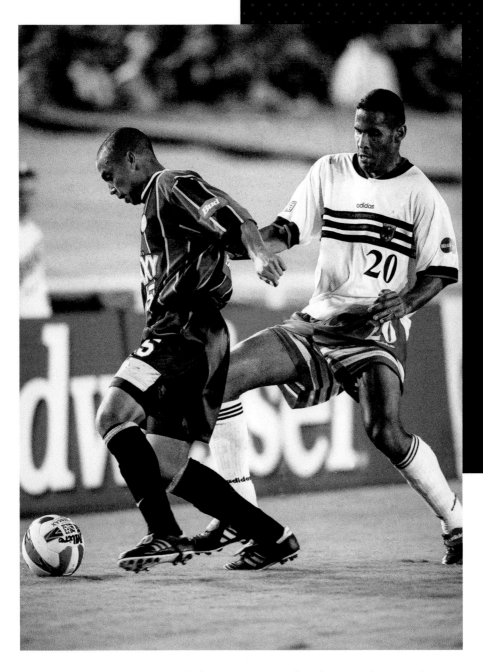

Tony Sanneh (20) was one of the many US national team players who spent time with DC United.

Freddy Adu (9) makes his professional debut against San Jose in 2004.

WINNING A FOURTH CUP

After the 1999 MLS Cup win, the franchise weathered a
stretch of mediocre results. DC found its stride again in 2004,
however. That season did not start out smoothly. Injuries and
uneven play actually hurt the team through most of 2004. The
squad caught fire eventually, losing only two matches after
August 7. The late addition of Argentine midfielder Christian
Gómez propelled the team to the second seed in the playoffs.

SHOOTING STAR

DC United made headlines in November 2003 when the club signed Freddy Adu to a
six-year contract. Adu was a 14-year-old prodigy whose family had moved from Ghana
to the United States six years earlier. He made his first official appearance for the club
in April 2004. When he stepped on the field for the Black and Red, Adu became the
youngest professional athlete in any US team sport since 1887.

The expectations on Adu's shoulders were immense, as he was hailed as the
future of American soccer. He was called "the next Pelé" by soccer analysts and writers.
But that success never happened for Adu. After he struggled to live up to his early
promise, Adu was traded to Real Salt Lake in 2006. Though the young Adu did not
reach his potential in DC, the impact of his arrival brought MLS into the national sports
conversation, in many ways for the first time.

After getting past New England in a penalty shootout in the conference finals, DC faced Kansas City in the 2004 MLS Cup.

Though they fell behind 1–0, the Black and Red quickly stormed back. DC United responded with three straight goals in seven minutes. Two of the goals came from Alecko Eskandarian. With the 3–2 win over Kansas City, United won its fourth Cup in nine MLS seasons.

United won the Supporters' Shield for earning the most regular-season points in 2006 and 2007. But the team was knocked out of the playoffs before reaching the MLS Cup both years. Then it hit a dry spell, missing the playoffs in five of the next six years and setting a record for futility by winning just three league matches in 2013. Ironically, United won its third US Open Cup that year, defeating Real Salt Lake 1–0 in the final.

Fortunes changed in 2014 as the franchise experienced a worst-to-first turnaround under coach Ben Olsen. He had played 11 seasons for the Black and Red, retiring in 2009. He took over as the team's head coach during the 2010 season, aiming to return United to its glory days. DC's teams under Olsen were young, fast, and exciting. United's fanbase was energized once again as the squad won the Eastern Conference.

Construction of DC United's new stadium was completed in 2018.

Although another MLS Cup victory remained elusive, United took a bold step into the future in 2018. Following more than a decade of trying to secure a new stadium, United moved to Audi Field on July 14, 2018. The state-of-the-art venue was built in the Buzzard Point section of the city, not far from the home stadium of baseball's Washington Nationals. The team that set the standard in the early years of MLS finally had a high-end, modern stadium to call home.

CHAPTER 3

BLACK AND
RED STARS

DC United's history of excellence began with the team's first coach, Bruce Arena. He arrived in DC after serving the same role for the University of Virginia's men's soccer team. Arena worked quickly, establishing the first MLS dynasty, but he didn't stick around long. Arena left DC United in 1998 for one of the most important jobs in American soccer: coach of the US men's national team.

DC United has always had its share of talent. Bolivians Jaime Moreno and Marco Etcheverry led the charge during the early dynasty. Etcheverry was one of the most dominant midfielders in MLS history. Many observers consider him DC United's best player ever. Etcheverry joined DC United in 1996, and his offense was one of the main reasons for the

Bruce Arena receives a gift from two of his star players, Marco Etcheverry (10) and John Harkes, as he prepared to leave to coach the US men's national team in 1998.

team's victories in back-to-back MLS Cups. Etcheverry had an even better 1998 season, when he was named the league MVP. He finished his career in DC with 191 appearances, 34 goals, and 101 assists. As a final feather in his cap, Etcheverry was named as one of MLS' 25 greatest players of all time in 2020.

Moreno was part of four MLS Cups in the nation's capital. He is also remembered as one of the key pieces of DC United's early success. Moreno earned a spot on the MLS All-Star team seven times as a member of DC United. He made the Best XI four times and was later named one of MLS' 25 greatest players ever. Through the 2020 season, Moreno and Landon Donovan are the only MLS players with 100 career goals and 100 career assists.

AMERICAN TRIO

US national team stalwarts Eddie Pope, John Harkes, and Jeff Agoos were also indispensable during DC's dynasty. Pope was

Jeff Agoos (12) carries the trophy after DC United won the inaugural MLS Cup in 1996. He's flanked by teammates John Harkes (6), Tony Sanneh (20), Raúl Díaz Arce (21), and Shawn Medved (13).

known as one of the most tenacious defenders in MLS history. He was a part of three MLS Cup championships in DC. Pope's top season came in 1997 when he earned MLS Defender of the Year. He also made his first of four Best XI Teams in 1997. Pope played his last game in DC in 2002 after seven seasons with the Black and Red.

Eddie Pope, *right*, was a strong defender for United and the US national team.

In 1992 midfielder Harkes became the first American to play in England's first division. He remained in England until 1996, when he became the first player signed to DC United's roster. He was a vital leader for the Black and Red during the 1996 MLS Cup run. Harkes also assisted on the winning goal in the 1997 MLS Cup. This play cemented him as one of the most memorable players in franchise history.

25 FOR 25

In 2020 MLS celebrated its 25th season by naming its 25 greatest players. Of those 25 players, six had played for DC United: Jeff Agoos, Dwayne De Rosario, Marco Etcheverry, Jaime Moreno, Eddie Pope, and Nick Rimando.

Agoos was another important American on the early United teams. Agoos, with Pope, led a suffocating defense on three MLS Cup champion teams. Agoos's rugged style helped United control the midfield. He represented DC United five times in the All-Star Game. Agoos made the Best XI Team three times and in 2020 was named one of MLS' 25 greatest players ever. His final honor for the Black and Red came in 2008 when he was inducted into the team's Hall of Tradition.

They were hardly the only American stars for DC United in its early years, though. Defenders Carlos Llamosa and Tony Sanneh, midfielders Richie Williams and Ben Olsen, and forward Roy Lassiter were all US national team regulars at some point.

PLAYER, COACH, ICON

Ben Olsen is arguably the most important figure in DC United history. Olsen played midfield for the Black and Red from 1998 to 2009. He helped DC win MLS Cups in 1999 and 2004. Olsen was especially important during the team's 1999 season, as he scored five goals and had 11 assists. He was also named the MVP of the 1999 MLS Cup. At the end of his playing career, Olsen was among the franchise leaders in games played and game-winning goals.

Olsen then became head coach of DC United in the middle of the 2010 season. At the time he was the youngest head coach in MLS history at 33 years old. Over the next decade he led the team to the playoffs six times and became the longest-tenured coach in team history.

Olsen's best season as a coach came in 2014. United jumped from 16 points in 2013 to 59 points the next year. This marked the biggest single-season turnaround in MLS history. Olsen took home the MLS Coach of the Year Award in 2014, adding to the eight trophies he earned as a player. In 2019 Olsen became the youngest coach in league history to record 100 wins.

Ben Olsen, *right*, made his mark on the franchise as a player and coach.

Wayne Rooney brought talent and intensity to DC when he arrived from England in 2018.

However, with the team struggling late in the 2020 season, the team fired Olsen.

"It is a unique road, going from a player and being a coach for this long in this day and age in sports," Olsen said. "It just doesn't happen that often. I feel lucky I was one of the rare ones to go this way. Of course, I wish we had had more success."

WAYNE ROONEY

After missing the playoffs in 2017, DC United was in need of a spark. Wayne Rooney provided it. Rooney, the all-time leading scorer from England's national team, arrived in DC that summer. He formed a potent partnership with Luciano Acosta to make Audi Field's first season a memorable one. Rooney scored 12 goals in his first season and 11 in his second, leading the team both years. United reached the playoffs both years, too. However, Rooney's time in DC ended before most fans would have liked. He went back to England to serve as a player-coach at Derby County for the 2019–20 season.

CHAPTER 4

UNITED IN
EXCELLENCE

DC United has had a number of big moments over the years. But few can compare to their four MLS Cup victories. In 1997 coach Bruce Arena believed the team's deep lineup was its strongest attribute. United started its championship defense strong, winning its first four games. Raúl Díaz Arce and Jaime Moreno combined for four goals during the 4–0 start.

DC went on to win 21 games in 97, totaling 55 points in the standings. This mark earned United the league's Supporter's Shield. Their playoffs began against the New England Revolution. DC United continued its offensive onslaught with two goals apiece from Moreno and striker Roy Wegerle. They dominated New England, winning by a score of 4–1. In Game 2 of the best-of-three series, DC faced a

Jaime Moreno had a strong showing for DC United during the 1997 playoffs.

stiffer challenge. The match went back and forth, but as usual, United came up big when it mattered most. Tied 1–1 after 120 minutes, United won the shootout 4–3 to take the series and advance to the Eastern Conference finals.

DC's next opponent was the Columbus Crew. In Game 1 at RFK Stadium, Tony Sanneh scored twice as the Black and Red stormed out to a 3–0 lead. United held on for a 3–2 victory. Game 2 in Columbus was a test. Facing elimination, Columbus gave DC its best shot in a physical, hard-fought match. Both teams' defenses were primed and allowed few scoring chances in the first half. Díaz Arce struck early in the second half, giving DC a 1–0 lead. It was the 17th goal of his memorable second season with DC United. Díaz Arce's strike and a stingy defense proved to be enough on that day. A chance at a second straight MLS cup awaited the Black and Red.

The stage was set for the winner-take-all MLS Cup against Colorado in 1997. RFK served as the venue. DC United's rabid fanbase didn't disappoint, as the title game's attendance was the largest in franchise history at the time. Like the MLS Cup the season before, the weather was a factor. RFK's field was soggy due to heavy rain.

Team members celebrate after DC United won the 1997 MLS Cup against Colorado.

The match started out sloppily, with each team trying to find its footing. In the 37th minute, Jaime Moreno capped off his brilliant 1997 season with his 19th goal. Sanneh struck again for DC in the 68th minute. On the other side, Colorado's chances were neutralized by Eddie Pope at the head of a ferocious defense. Colorado managed to score a goal, but it was too little, too late. DC United earned its second MLS Cup in two seasons.

DROUGHT, THEN MORE SUCCESS

The Black and Red won a third cup in 1999. But then they hit a rough spot before climbing back to the top in 2004. After an inconsistent start to the regular season, the team got it together just in time and surged into the playoffs.

After racing past the New York/New Jersey MetroStars in the conference semifinals, United faced the New England Revolution in the conference finals. United hosted the game at RFK Stadium in front of a raucous DC crowd. The field was sprinkled with stars as both teams boasted a mix of young and experienced talent. Both squads were also hitting their strides at the right time, setting up a classic. Something had to give at RFK.

The action was fast right from the start. In the 11th minute, United forward Alecko Eskandarian scored with an assist from Olsen. New England equalized, only to watch Moreno put DC ahead again. The back-and-forth pace continued as New England scored the tying goal in the 44th minute, sending the game to the halftime break 2–2.

Christian Gómez gave United the advantage again in the 67th minute with an improbable header from the left side. But the epic match would not end without a final twist. With only

DC United goalkeeper Nick Rimando, *back*, battles for the ball against New England's Jay Heaps during the 2004 Eastern Conference final.

five minutes left in the match, New England tied the game yet again. A match like this just had to be settled by a shootout.

With the suspense at its peak, both teams missed their first penalty kicks. After five rounds, the shootout was still tied.

Alecko Eskandarian, *left*, and Jaime Moreno celebrate after Eskandarian's second goal against Kansas City during the 2004 MLS Cup.

American midfielder Brian Carroll stepped in to take the next shot for DC. Carroll had not scored a single goal that season. He shot the ball into the top left corner of the net to give DC a 4–3 lead.

In a match filled with huge plays, United keeper Nick Rimando made the biggest one of all. Rimando guessed right and punched away New England's final penalty kick. DC United went on to beat Kansas City 3–2 in the MLS Cup. But the conference final match against New England has been called the best game in MLS history.

ROONEY ARRIVES

With the team in another title drought, United raised the stakes by signing English superstar Wayne Rooney. The former Manchester United captain was known as a fierce competitor and a dangerous forward who seemingly scored at will. Rooney already held the scoring record for both Manchester United and England's national team. And at age 32, he still had plenty of gas left in the tank.

Rooney made his DC debut on July 14, 2018, the same day Audi Field opened. It was a huge day for the club, and the players responded with a 3–1 victory over Vancouver. Rooney scored his first goal for his new club two weeks later against Colorado. It was his first game after being named team captain. But his time in the United States might be best remembered for a remarkable play he made on August 12 against Orlando City.

The match was tied 2–2 at the end of 90 minutes, but the officials added six minutes of stoppage time. As those six minutes were about to run out, Rooney showed his value on both ends of the field. First, Orlando City's Will Johnson broke free with the ball near midfield, hoping to launch one last attack for his side. However, Rooney ran him down and made a clean slide tackle, sending the ball rolling toward the sideline as Johnson tumbled to the ground.

But Rooney wasn't done. He hopped up, gathered the ball, and headed back the other way. He dribbled past midfield and toward the Orlando goal when he launched a long, arcing cross into the box. The ball just cleared a defender and landed on the head of United's Luciano Acosta. His header beat the Orlando keeper for his third goal of the match, putting United on top 3–2 in the 96th minute.

The goal touched off a wild celebration in the Audi Field stands. Acosta jumped onto a barrier and rejoiced with fans as he was swarmed by his teammates. Rooney appeared nonchalant about it all, however, as though it was the type of play he expected of himself.

United finished the season with seven wins and three draws in its final 10 matches to roar into the playoffs. Rooney led

Wayne Rooney, *center*, celebrates with his teammates after DC United won his debut and the team's first game at Audi Field on July 14, 2018.

the team back to the postseason in 2019 before returning to England. He might not have delivered a trophy to United. But DC fans will be talking about that remarkable long ball against Orlando for years to come.

TIMELINE

1996	1996	1997	1999	2004

⌄	⌄	⌄	⌄	⌄
DC United loses at San Jose 1–0 in the first match in MLS history on April 6.	United closes out the season by winning the first MLS Cup in a 3–2 defeat of the LA Galaxy on October 20.	United makes it back-to-back MLS Cup titles by defeating the Colorado Rapids 2–1 on October 26.	For the third time in four years, DC United are MLS Cup champions after beating the Galaxy 2–0 on November 21.	United wins its fourth MLS Cup, with a 3–2 win over Kansas City on November 14.

2007	2010	2012	2017	2018

⌄	⌄	⌄	⌄	⌄
The club earns its second consecutive Supporters' Shield after going 16–7–7 in the regular season.	Less than a year after retiring, longtime United star Ben Olsen is named interim head coach.	DC United returns to the MLS playoffs for the first time in five seasons.	The final home game at RFK Stadium is played on October 22.	Wayne Rooney debuts in the first game at Audi Field on July 14.

TEAM FACTS

FIRST SEASON

1996

STADIUMS

RFK Stadium (1996–2017)
Audi Field (2018–)

MLS CUP TITLES

1996, 1997, 1999, 2004

US OPEN CUP TITLES

1996, 2008, 2013

CONCACAF CHAMPIONS LEAGUE TITLES

1998

KEY PLAYERS

Jeff Agoos (1996–2000)
Bobby Boswell (2005–07, 2014–17)
Dwayne De Rosario (2011–13)
Raúl Díaz Arce (1996–97, 2000–01)
Luciano Emilio (2007–10)
Marco Etcheverry (1996–2003)
Christian Gómez (2004–07, 2009)
Bill Hamid (2010–)
John Harkes (1996–98)
Jaime Moreno (1996–2002, 2004–10)
Ben Olsen (1998–2009)
Eddie Pope (1996–2002)
Wayne Rooney (2018–19)
Richie Williams (1996–2000, 2002)

KEY COACHES

Bruce Arena (1996–98)
Piotr Nowak (2004–06)
Ben Olsen (2010–20)
Thomas Rongen (1999–2001)
Tom Soehn (2007–09)

MLS MOST VALUABLE PLAYERS

Dwayne De Rosario (2011)
Luciano Emilio (2007)
Marco Etcheverry (1998)
Christian Gómez (2006)

MLS DEFENDER OF THE YEAR

Bobby Boswell (2006)
Eddie Pope (1997)

MLS NEWCOMER OF THE YEAR

Luciano Emilio (2007)

MLS GOALKEEPER OF THE YEAR

Bill Hamid (2014)
Troy Perkins (2006)

MLS ROOKIE OF THE YEAR

Andy Najar (2010)
Ben Olsen (1998)

MLS COACH OF THE YEAR

Bruce Arena (1997)
Ben Olsen (2014)

GLOSSARY

assist
A pass that leads directly to a goal.

cross
A pass delivered from the side of the field toward the middle.

dynasty
A team that has an extended period of success, usually winning multiple championships in the process.

equalize
To tie the score in a soccer match.

golden goal
A goal scored in added extra time to win a game under a sudden-death format.

playoffs
A set of games played after the regular season that decides which team is the champion.

prodigy
A young player who has a great natural ability for a sport.

shootout
A tiebreaking shootout after stoppage time to decide who wins a game.

slide tackle
The act of sliding underneath a player to take the ball away.

stoppage time
Also known as added time, a number of minutes tacked onto the end of a half for stoppages that occurred during play from injuries, free kicks, and goals.

substitute
A player who does not start the match but who enters later to replace a teammate.

MORE
INFORMATION

BOOKS

Karpovich, Todd. *Manchester United*. Minneapolis, MN: Abdo Publishing, 2018

Kortemeier, Todd. *Total Soccer*. Minneapolis, MN: Abdo Publishing, 2017.

Marthaler, Jon. *MLS*. Minneapolis, MN: Abdo Publishing, 2020.

ONLINE RESOURCES

To learn more about DC United, please visit
abdobooklinks.com or scan this QR code. These links are
routinely monitored and updated to provide the most current
information available.

INDEX

ABOUT THE AUTHOR

Sam Moussavi is a novelist and freelance writer based in the San Francisco Bay Area. He has written two sets of young adult novels as well as many nonfiction sports titles.